DREAMWORKS

GABBY'S DOLLHOUSE

Kitty Fairy's Garden Magic

Adapted by Gabhi Martins

DreamWorks Gabby's Dollhouse © 2022 DreamWorks Animation LLC. All Rights Reserved.

All rights reserved. Published by Scholastic Inc., *Publishers since 1920.* SCHOLASTIC and associated logos are trademarks and/or registered trademarks of Scholastic Inc.

The publisher does not have any control over and does not assume any responsibility for author or third-party websites or their content.

No part of this publication may be reproduced, stored in a retrieval system, or transmitted in any form or by any means, electronic, mechanical, photocopying, recording, or otherwise, without written permission of the publisher. For information regarding permission, write to Scholastic Inc., Attention: Permissions Department, 557 Broadway, New York, NY 10012.

This book is a work of fiction. Names, characters, places, and incidents are either the product of the author's imagination or are used fictitiously, and any resemblance to actual persons, living or dead, business establishments, events, or locales is entirely coincidental.

ISBN 978-1-338-79275-1

10 9 8 7 6 5 4 3 2 1   22 23 24 25 26

Printed in the U.S.A.   40

First printing 2022

Book design by Salena Mahina

Scholastic Inc.

A Dollhouse delivery came today in the most interesting box! Let's see what's inside.

A-meow-zing! There's a small bag of dirt, a tiny watering can, a mini pot, and an itty bitty, teeny-weeny seed. The seed is sparkly!

What will grow from the sparkly seed? If I plant it, it'll take weeks for the seed to sprout.

I need the help of Kitty Fairy! I bet she could help my new seed sprout right away.

It's time to get tiny!

In the Fairy Tail Garden, Kitty Fairy flies over to Pandy Paws and me. "What's in this adorable little pot?" she asks.

"It's a sparkly seed surprise," I explain. "Can you make it grow super fast?"

"You know I can," Kitty Fairy says. "It'll just take . . . a little garden magic!"

Kitty Fairy makes a tiny magic rain cloud appear. It sprinkles water into the pot.

It doesn't take long before Kitty Fairy notices something plant-tastic. The sparkly seed sprouted!

Pandy Paws peers into the pot. It's a little-bitty baby flower!

"It's an Itty Bitty Blossom!" Kitty Fairy explains. "She's small now, but Itty Bitty Blossoms become fully grown in just one day."

"Until she's fully grown, you need to take care of her just like any other baby," Kitty Fairy explains.

Just then, Itty Bitty Blossom starts sobbing!

"Don't cry," Pandy Paws says. "Our itty bitty flower must need something. I have plenty of purr-rific things in my Pandy Pack that could help!"

Pandy Paws tries bubbles.

Then he shares his squishy toy.

But Itty Bitty Blossom keeps crying. "I don't know what else to do!" Pandy Paws says.

Pandy Paws is about to give up. Just then, Itty Bitty Blossom pops Pandy Paws's thumb into her mouth.

"She must be hungry!" Kitty Fairy says. She flies over with a milk plant.

Itty Bitty Blossom finishes her milk. But then she starts crying again!

My baby cousins need to burp after they eat. Maybe Itty Bitty Blossom does, too! But how do I burp her?

Kitty Fairy knows just who to ask. "Mama Box will know what to do!" she says.

As we leave, Kitty Fairy cries out, "Remember to bring her back before she outgrows her pot!"

In the craft room, Pandy Paws introduces our new friend to Mama and Baby Box. "This is Itty Bitty Blossom. We fed her and now she really needs to burp!"

"You need a plant burper!" Mama Box says. "We can make one. Let's get crafting!"

Together, we make a cat-tastic burper. It gently pats Itty Bitty Blossom on the back. In no time, she is happily burping.

Itty Bitty Blossom should feel better, but she's still upset. What does she need now?

Pandy Paws and I take Itty Bitty Blossom to see MerCat.

"Itty Bitty Blossom is sprouting thorns on her stem," MerCat says. "Like when a baby gets new teeth."

Ouch! How can we help her thorny stems?

"We need a special sea sponge," MerCat says. I turn my hair into seaweed and use it to catch a sponge.

The sea sponge spray soothes Itty Bitty Blossom's thorns.

Now Itty Bitty Blossom is tired, but she can't fall asleep. Luckily, we know just the cat to help her take a nap.

In the music room, Pandy Paws asks DJ Catnip for help. "Do you know any lullabies for plants?"

"I've sung lots of things to sleep," says DJ Catnip. "But I'll need to write a special song for this plant!"

DJ Catnip sings a purr-rific tune. She falls right asleep.

When Itty Bitty Blossom wakes up, she's no longer crying. But there is a new problem. She's growing!

Pandy Paws notices cracks in her pot. "We need to get back to the Fairy Tail Garden!" he says. "Let's call Carlita!"

Carlita zooms into the music room to pick us up. "To the Fairy Tail Garden, please!" I say.

"Hop in!" Carlita says.

We get to the garden just in time. I plant Itty Bitty Blossom in the ground, and she grows to her full size!

"I think we should call her Biggie Blossom now!" I say.

"She'll always be a baby in my eyes!" Pandy Paws says.